Raggedy Ann
and the Kittens
and other toy stories

Compiled by Tig Thomas

Miles
Kelly

First published in 2014 by Miles Kelly Publishing Ltd
Harding's Barn, Bardfield End Green, Thaxted, Essex, CM6 3PX, UK

2 4 6 8 10 9 7 5 3 1

Publishing Director Belinda Gallagher
Creative Director Jo Cowan
Editorial Director Rosie Neave
Senior Editor Sarah Parkin
Senior Designer Joe Jones
Production Manager Elizabeth Collins
Reprographics Stephan Davis, Jennifer Hunt, Thom Allaway

ISBN 978-1-78209-463-0

Printed in China

British Library Cataloguing-in-Publication Data
A catalogue record for this book is available from the British Library

ACKNOWLEDGEMENTS

The publishers would like to thank the following artists who have contributed to this book:

Advocate Art: Claire Keay, Bruno Merz, Eva Sassin (cover), Kimberley Scott
Beehive Illustration: Rupert Van Wyk (inc. decorative frames)

Made with paper from a sustainable forest

www.mileskelly.net   info@mileskelly.net

Contents

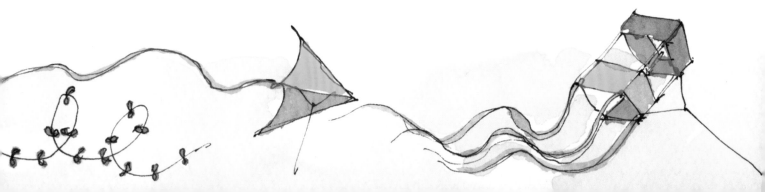

The Kite Tells his Tale

By Frances Freeling Broderip

AT TEATIME, one summer evening, Mamma said to the children, "Tomorrow Uncle Gee is coming!" They all burst out in one shout of delight, for Uncle Gee was their favourite uncle, and always ready for fun and games.

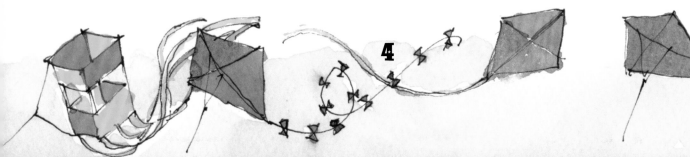

And the next day, Uncle Gee came, to the great delight of the children. But, to their horror, they looked out and saw the sky covered with clouds, and heard the steady, heavy drops of rain falling.

"What a nuisance," growled Bob and Tom, "when Uncle Gee promised to have a game of cricket with us!"

"O dear," said Mary, "and I wanted to show him the new hammock swing!"

"Rain, rain, go to Spain," chanted Baby.

"What's the matter now?" said Uncle Gee, coming in. "All this racket about a little rain! Why, I was just thinking what a day it would be to make a kite!"

"Make a kite!" shouted Bob. "Oh Uncle Gee, can you show us how to do it?"

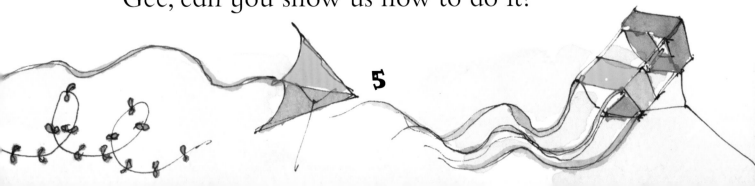

5

"I think I can, Bob," replied his uncle. And when breakfast was over, to work they all went. Papa found some slips of light thin wood and lent his best knife. Mamma gave some beautiful white material to cover the frame with, and her glue pot as well. Uncle Gee soon had the long table covered with all sorts of things and had set everybody to work.

"Now," said Uncle Gee, "Mary, you and Jeanie can find me some strips of coloured paper for the tail, and Dora, you get me a long ball of string."

glue

And so the work went on, Bob and Tom helping Uncle Gee, and Mary and Jeanie supplying the long piece of string, provided for the tail, with its cross pieces of paper to serve as light weights. They busily snipped some fine red paper in order to make a grand tassel to finish the tail with.

"The kite is getting beautifully dry and tight," said Uncle Gee, as he took his place at dinner. "What shall we make it? A flying dragon, like the Chinese flags and lanterns?"

"Oh yes! Uncle Gee," cried Dora, "do make it a dragon — a green

7

dragon with a fiery tail!"

"A fairy with wings," suggested Mary, "with a star on her forehead."

"Or a ship," said Jeanie. "A ship with masts and sails painted for her, because you know she does sail through the air, Uncle Gee!"

"Paint it like a daisy," said Baby, "or make buttercups all over it!"

"Well, we'll see," said Uncle Gee. "When dinner is over we'll have a solemn council on the matter, and the most votes shall carry the day."

After dinner, they found the great kite very dry, and nice and flat it was too. They were all delighted with it.

"Now," said Uncle Gee, "once and for all

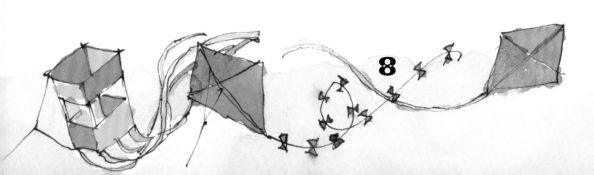

what is it to be? A ship, a dragon or what? It is to be put to the vote – what do you say?"

And so there was a great deal of talking and chattering among them all, and at last the children agreed to ask Uncle Gee to make the kite a bird.

"But we can't settle what kind of bird it is to be," said Bob. "I wanted an eagle, but Tom liked an owl better, and Mary said she liked a dove, while Jeanie said it must be a peacock. Dora wanted a swan, and Baby bawled out for a robin! So you must decide out of all the number, Uncle Gee."

"All right," was Uncle Gee's reply, and to work he went. He painted away while the children all looked on and made remarks as he sketched in the outline. But they began

9

to press round him, so Uncle Gee declared he would not do another stroke till they left him alone. So off they went to the other end of the table, and got the tail in order.

By the time that the tail was finished, Uncle Gee had completed the kite. Turning it round to the children, he showed a bird of such a kind as had never been seen before! It had the head of an owl, with its great staring eyes, the broad wings of an eagle, the neck of a dove, the breast of a robin, the many-eyed tail of a peacock, and the webbed feet of a swan!

The children gazed

at it for a moment in utter surprise, and then they all burst into shouts of approval.

"There," said Uncle Gee, "I hope I have satisfied you all. I am sure such a bird as this would make its fortune in a zoo!"

"Oh! What a jolly fellow!" shouted Bob and Tom, clapping their hands, while the girls danced round quite delighted.

"Now," said Uncle Gee, "I think tomorrow will be a fine day after the rain, and we shall be able to make this fine fellow fly."

So they tied on my tail and made me thoroughly ready for the next morning's cruise. Then

11

they all went to bed the happiest set of little ones within fifty miles around.

Many a flight I had with them over field, meadow and moor, and many a tree have I got entangled with. At last, Bob became quite expert at climbing trees, and all owing to the practise he had in getting me.

So here you have an end of my history, which contains, as you see now, no flying adventures at all. If I had time, I could tell you of many curious things I saw in my airy flights, and some about the clouds I went so near, but I must leave that until another day.

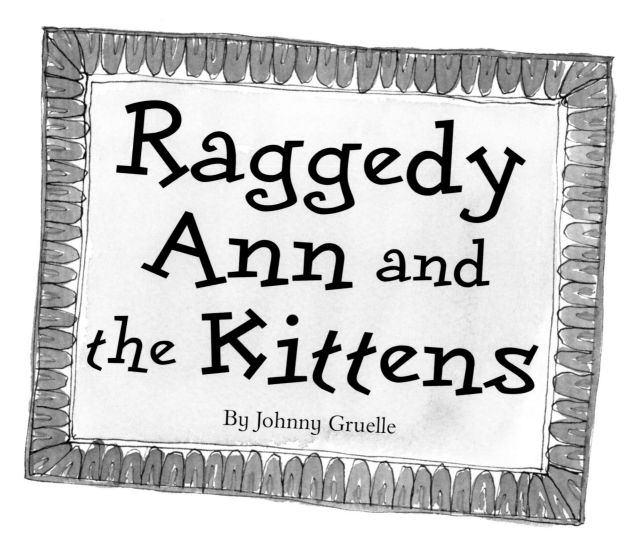

Raggedy Ann and the Kittens

By Johnny Gruelle

Marcella owns a whole set of toys, including a soldier doll, Uncle Clem, two tiny dolls called penny dolls, and her beloved rag doll called Raggedy Ann. Fido is her dog.

MARCELLA HAD COME EARLY in the morning and dressed all the dolls and placed them about the nursery. Some of the dolls had been put in the little red chairs around the little doll table.

There was nothing to eat upon the table except a turkey, a fried egg and an apple, all painted in natural colours. The little teapot and other doll dishes were empty, but Marcella had told them to enjoy their dinner while she was away.

The French doll had been given a seat upon the doll sofa and Uncle Clem had been placed at the piano. Marcella picked up Raggedy Ann and carried her out of the nursery when she left, telling the dolls to "be real good children."

When the door closed, the tin soldier winked at the Dutch-boy doll.

"Shall I play you a tune?" Uncle Clem asked the French doll.

At this all the dolls laughed, for Uncle

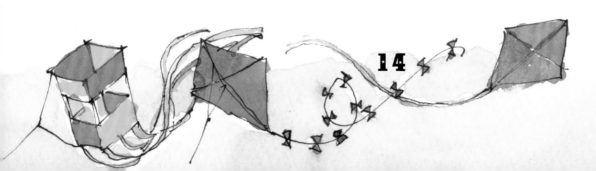

Clem could not play any tune. Raggedy Ann was the only doll who had ever taken lessons, and she could play 'Peter Peter Pumpkin Eater' with one hand. In fact, Marcella had almost worn out Raggedy Ann's right hand teaching it to her!

"Yes, play something lively!" said the French doll.

So Uncle Clem began hammering the eight keys on the toy piano with all his might. But then, a noise was suddenly heard upon the stairs.

Quick as a wink, all the dolls took the same positions in which they had been placed by Marcella that morning, for they did not wish people to know that they could move about.

But it was only Fido. He put his nose in the door and looked around.

All the dolls at the table looked steadily at the painted food. Uncle Clem leaned upon the piano keys, looking just like he had when he had been placed there.

"I've found something I must tell Raggedy Ann about," Fido said excitedly. "It's kittens!"

"How lovely!" cried all the dolls. "Real live kittens?"

"Real live kittens!" replied Fido. "Three tiny ones, out in the barn!"

"Oh, I wish Raggedy Ann was here,"

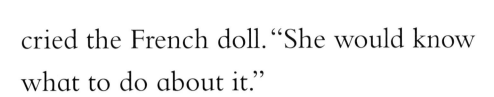

cried the French doll. "She would know what to do about it."

"That's why I wanted to see her," said Fido. "I did not know there were any kittens and I went into the barn to hunt for mice. Mamma Cat came bouncing right at me! I knew there must be something inside or she would not have jumped at me that way," Fido continued. "And I found three tiny kittens in an old basket in a dark corner."

"Go get them, Fido, and bring them up so we can see them," said the tin soldier.

"Not me!" said Fido. "If I had a suit of tin clothes on like you have I might do it, but you know cats can scratch very hard."

"We will tell Raggedy Ann when she comes in," said the French doll.

When Raggedy Ann had been returned to the nursery, the dolls could hardly wait until Marcella had put on their nighties and left them for the night. Then they quickly told Raggedy Ann all about the kittens.

Raggedy Ann suggested that all the dolls go out to the barn and see the kittens. This they did easily, for the window was open and it was but a short jump to the ground.

They found Fido out near the barn, watching a hole.

"I was afraid something might disturb them," he said, "for Mamma Cat went away about an hour ago."

All the dolls crawled through the hole and ran to the basket.

Just as Raggedy Ann started to pick up

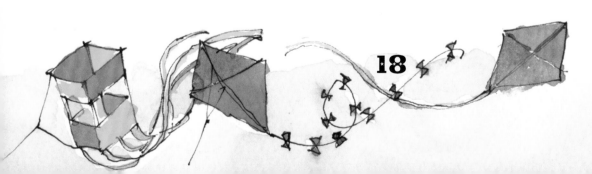

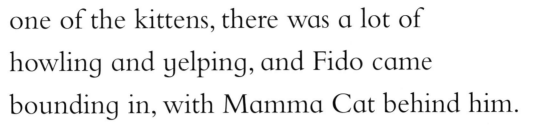

one of the kittens, there was a lot of howling and yelping, and Fido came bounding in, with Mamma Cat behind him.

"I'm surprised at you, Mamma Cat," said Raggedy Ann. "Fido has been watching your kittens while you were away. He would not hurt them for anything."

"I'm sorry, then," said Mamma Cat.

"Have you told the folks up at the house about your kittens?" Raggedy Ann asked.

"No!" exclaimed Mamma Cat. "At the last place I lived the people found out about my kittens and they all disappeared!"

"But all the folks at this house are very kind people and would love your kittens," cried all the dolls.

"Let's take them right up to the nursery,"

19

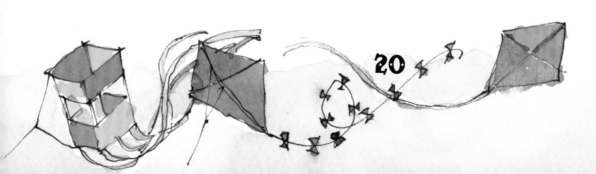

said Raggedy Ann, "and Mistress can find them there in the morning."

"How lovely!" said all the dolls in chorus. "Do, Mamma Cat!"

So after a great deal of persuasion, Mamma Cat agreed. Raggedy Ann took two of the kittens and carried them to the house, and Mamma Cat carried the other.

Raggedy Ann wanted to give the kittens her bed, but Fido insisted that Mamma Cat and the kittens should have his soft basket.

The dolls could hardly sleep that night, they were so anxious to see what Mistress would say when she found the dear little kittens in the morning.

When Marcella came to the nursery, the first thing she saw was the three little

20

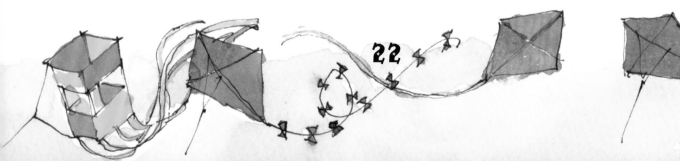

kittens. She cried out in delight and carried them all down to show to Mamma and Daddy. They said the kittens could stay in the nursery and belong to Marcella.

Marcella finally decided upon three names – Prince Charming for the white kitten, Cinderella for the tabby, and Princess Golden for the kitten with yellow stripes.

So that is how the three little kittens came to live in the nursery. And Mamma Cat found out that Fido was a very good friend, too. She grew to trust him so much she would even let him help to wash the kittens' faces!

A Family Christmas

An extract from *What Katy Did*
by Susan Coolidge

*Katy Carr has hurt her back and has to stay in bed,
but her brothers and sisters always try to make her part of the fun.
She is talking about Christmas plans for the children with
her aunt, who looks after her.*

I THOUGHT OF such a nice plan yesterday," Katy said. "It was that all of them should hang their stockings up here tomorrow night instead of in the nursery. Then I could see them open their presents.

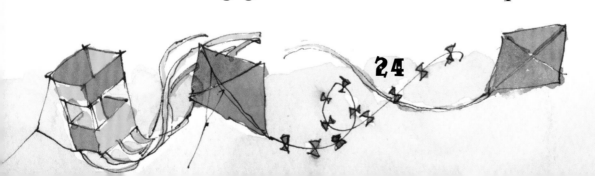

Could they, Aunt Izzie? It would be fun."

"I don't believe there will be any objection," replied her aunt. She looked as if she were trying not to laugh.

"I wish I had something pretty for everybody," Katy went on, wistfully. "There's my pink sash," she said suddenly. "I might give that to Clover. Would you please fetch it and let me see, Aunt Izzie? It's in the top drawer."

Aunt Izzie brought the sash. It proved to be quite fresh.

"I wish I had something nice for Elsie. What she wants most of all is a writing desk," Katy said. "And Johnnie wants a sled. But, oh dear! These are such big things. And I've only got two dollars and a quarter."

Aunt Izzie marched out of the room. When she came back she had something folded up in her hand.

"I didn't know what to give you for Christmas, Katy," she said. "So I thought I'd give you this, and let you choose for yourself. But perhaps you'd rather have it now." So saying, Aunt Izzie laid on the bed a crisp, new five-dollar bill!

"How good you are!" cried Katy.

She gave Aunt Izzie an exact description of the desk she wanted.

"It's no matter about its being very big," said Katy, "but it must have a blue velvet lining, and an inkstand with a silver top. Oh! And there must be a lock and key. Don't forget that, Aunt Izzie."

"No, I won't. What else?"

"I'd like the sled to be green," continued Katy, "and to have a nice name. If there's enough money left, Aunty, would you buy me a nice book for Dorry and another for Cecy, and a silver thimble for Mary? Oh! And some candy. And something for Debby and Bridget. I think that's all!"

Was ever seven dollars and a quarter expected to do so much? Indeed, Aunt Izzie must have been a witch to make it hold out. But she did, and next day all the precious bundles came home.

"I got 'Snow Skimmer'," said Aunt Izzie.

"It's beautiful," said Katy.

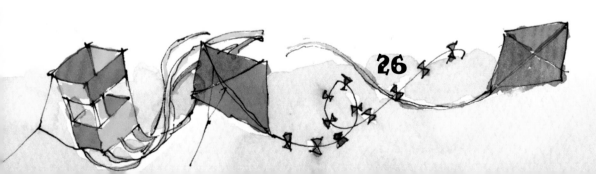

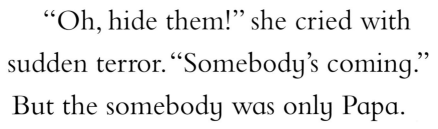

"Oh, hide them!" she cried with sudden terror. "Somebody's coming." But the somebody was only Papa.

These secrets took up so much of her thoughts that Katy scarcely found time to wonder at the absence of the children, who had hardly been seen. However, after supper they all came up.

"You don't know what we've been doing," began Philly.

"Hush, Phil!" said Clover. Then she divided the stockings that she held in her hand, and everybody hung them up.

Pretty soon Aunt Izzie came in and swept them all off to bed.

"You'll all be up as soon as it is light," she said, "so you must get your sleep now."

After they had gone, Katy recollected that nobody had offered to hang a stocking up for her. She felt a little hurt.

"But I suppose they forgot," she said to herself quietly.

Katy lay a long time watching the queer shapes of the stockings as they dangled in the firelight. Then she fell asleep.

It seemed only a minute before something touched her and woke her up. Behold, it was daytime, and there was Philly in his nightgown, climbing up on the bed to kiss her! The rest of the children, half dressed, were dancing about with their stockings in their hands.

"Merry Christmas!" they cried. "Oh Katy, such beautiful, beautiful things!"

"Oh!" shrieked Elsie, who at that moment spied her desk. "Santa Claus did bring it! Why, it's got 'from Katy' written on it! Oh Katy, I'm so happy!" Then Elsie hugged Katy and sobbed for pleasure.

But what was that strange thing beside the bed! Katy stared and rubbed her eyes. It certainly had not been there when she went to sleep. How had it got there?

It was a little evergreen tree planted in a red flowerpot. The pot had strips of paper stuck on it, and stars and crosses. The boughs of the tree were hung with oranges, nuts, shiny red apples, popcorn balls and strings of berries. There were also little packages tied with blue and crimson ribbon.

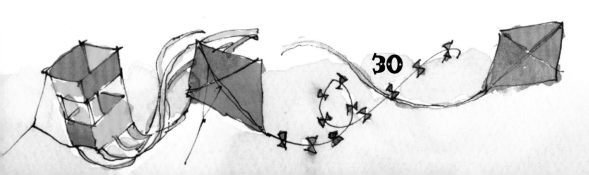

"It's a Christmas tree for you, because you're sick, you know!" said the children, all trying to hug her at once.

"We made it ourselves," said Dorry. "I pasted the black stars on the pot."

"And I popped the corn!" cried Philly.

"Do you like it?" asked Elsie, cuddling close to Katy. "That's my present – that one tied with a green ribbon. Don't you want to open them right away?"

Of course Katy wanted to. All sorts of things came out of the little bundles.

Elsie's present was a pen, with a grey kitten on it. Johnnie's, a doll's tea tray of scarlet tin. Dorry's gift, I regret to say, was a huge red-and-yellow spider, which whirred wildly when waved at the end of its string.

"They didn't want me to buy it," he said, "but I did! I thought it would amuse you. Does it amuse you, Katy?"

"Yes, indeed," said Katy, laughing and blinking as Dorry waved the spider to and fro before her eyes.

"How perfectly lovely everybody is!" said Katy, with grateful tears in her eyes.

That was a pleasant Christmas. The children declared it to be the nicest they had ever had. And though Katy couldn't quite say that, she enjoyed it too, and was very happy.

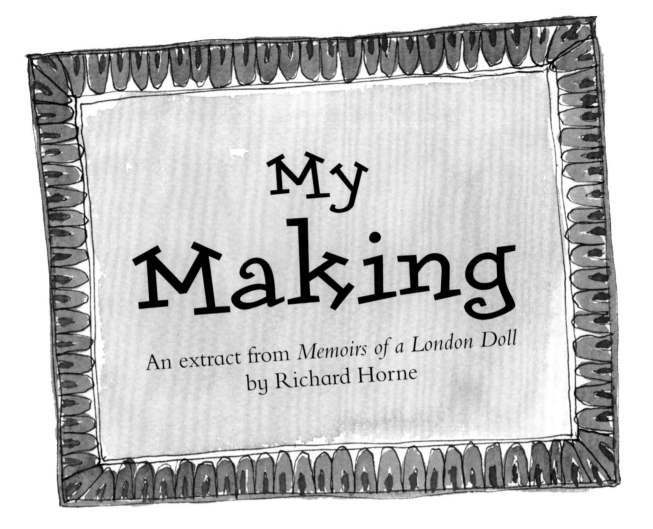

My Making

An extract from *Memoirs of a London Doll*
by Richard Horne

This tells the story of a Victorian wooden doll.

IN A LARGE, DUSKY ROOM, at the top of
a dusky house, there lived a poor doll-
maker, whose name was Sprat.

His bench was covered with little
wooden legs and arms, wooden heads
without hair, small bodies, half legs and half

arms, which had not yet been fitted together in the joints, paint pots and painting brushes, and bits of paper and rags of all colours.

All the family worked at doll-making. Mr Sprat was the great manager and doer of most things, and always the finisher, but Mrs Sprat painted the eyes, or else fitted in the glass ones. She also always painted the eyebrows. The eldest boy painted or glued hair onto the heads of the best dolls. The second boy fitted the legs and arms together. The little girl painted rosy cheeks and lips, which she always did very nicely, although sometimes she made them rather too red.

Now Mr Sprat was very clever. His usual

business was to make jointed dolls –
dolls that could move their legs and
arms in many positions, and these
were made of wood. This is what
I was made out of.

The first thing I remember was a
kind of a pegging and pushing and
scraping and twisting and tapping down
at both sides of me, above and below.

This was the fitting on of my legs and
arms. Next, my eyes were painted on and I
saw for the first time. Then I was passed into
the hands of the most gentle of all the Sprat
family, and felt something delightfully
warm laid upon my cheeks and mouth. It
was the little girl, who was painting me a
pair of rosy cheeks and lips, and her face, as

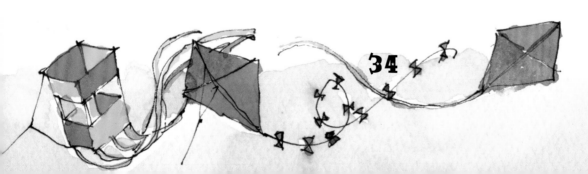

My Making

she bent over me, was the first thing that my eyes saw. The face was a smiling one, and as I looked up at it I tried to smile too, but I felt some hard material over the outside of my face.

But the last thing done to me was by Mr Sprat himself. He turned me around in his hands, examining and trying my legs and arms, which he moved backwards and forwards, and up and down. I was so frightened! I thought he would break something off me. However, nothing happened, and I was hung upon a line to dry, in the company of many other dolls, both boys and girls.

The tops of the beams were also covered

with dolls, all waiting there till their paint or varnish had properly dried and hardened.

Mr Sprat was a doll-maker only – he never made doll's clothes. So in about a week, when I was properly dry, Mr Sprat handed me to his wife. She wrapped me up in silver paper, all but my head, and laying me in a basket among nine others, she carried me off to a large doll shop.

"Place all these dolls on the shelf in the back parlour," said the master of the shop.

As I was carried to the shelf, I caught a glimpse of the shop window. Everything seemed so light! And then, I saw the large crowds of people passing outside in the world. Oh, how I longed to be placed in the shop window! I felt I should learn things so

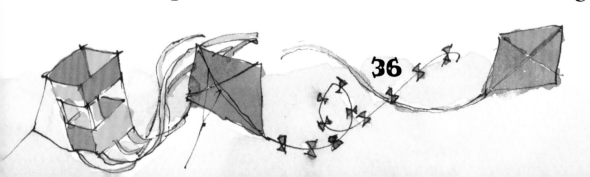

My Making

fast, if I could only see them.

But I was placed in a dark box, among a number of other dolls, for a long time. And when I was taken out, I was laid upon my back upon a high shelf, with my rosy cheeks and blue eyes turned upwards towards the ceiling.

How long I remained upon the shelf I do not know, but it seemed like years to me.

One day, however, the shop bell rang and a boy came in.

"If you please, sir," said the boy, "do you want a nice cake?"

"Not particularly," answered the master, "but I have no objection to one."

"I do not want any money for it, sir," said the boy.

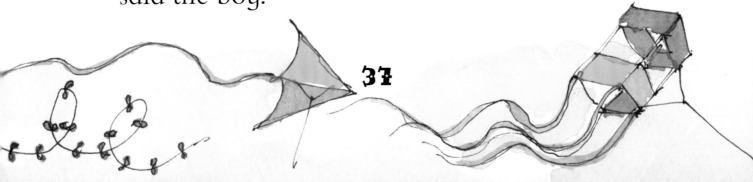

"What do you mean by that?" said the master of the shop.

"Why, sir," said the boy. "I want a nice doll for my sister, and I will give you this cake for a good doll."

"Let me see the cake," said the master. "How did you get it?"

"My grandfather is a baker, sir," answered the boy, "and my sister and I live with him. I went today to deliver seven cakes. But the family at one house had gone away and forgotten the cake, and grandfather told me that my sister and I might have it."

"What is your name?"

"Thomas Plummy, sir."

"Very well, Thomas Plummy, you may

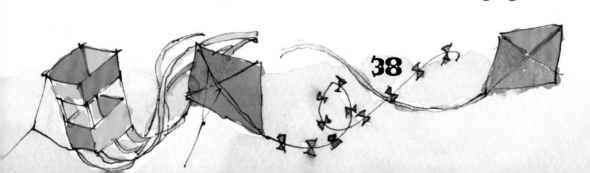

choose any doll you fancy out of that case."

Here some time passed as the boy went from one case to another, always refusing the dolls the master offered him, and when he did choose one himself, the master said it was too expensive.

Presently the master said he had another box full of good dolls in the back room, and in he came. But the boy had followed him to the door, and peeping in, suddenly called out, "There, sir! That one! That is the doll for my cake!" And he pointed his little brown finger up at me.

"Thomas Plummy!" said the master of the shop. "Take the doll and give me that cake. I only hope it may prove good."

"Thank you, sir," said the boy.

At the door he was met by his sister, who had been waiting to receive me in her arms.

That evening little Ellen Plummy begged to go to bed earlier than usual. She took me with her, and I had the great happiness of passing the whole night in the arms of my first mamma.